PUFFIN BOOKS

A CHRISTMAS CARD

'Whenever I see light feathers of snow moving slowly down a window ... and hear the thin moan of wind through casement cracks in a room where a fireplace is singing with flames, I remember the Christmas when I was nine, and our house at Indian Willows.'

It was Father's idea to spend Christmas in that lonely house in the woods near the eastern coast – a summer visitors' place where no one came in the winter. Driving down from the city, parents and the two young boys go hopelessly astray in the snow and dark. At last they find welcoming shelter for the night in a strange old mansion.

'No one has been here for quite a while,' said their host, a tall man in a cloak. 'This place is so far from anywhere that you have to be lost before you find it.' He is nowhere to be seen in the morning when they go, but he has left them a card – and it is the boy Marcel who first perceives that this card is a kind of map, what's more, a *living* map. First it shows the path to their house. But it has something more to tell. What is that point of light, always inching a little nearer? Can that dark shape be a man?

A wonderfully eerie story! Yet with moments of unforgettable brightness. And, as we come to see through the eyes of Marcel, as close to the spirit of Christmas as any modern tale we are likely to read.

Paul Theroux was born in 1941 in Medford, Massachusetts, and published his first book in 1967. He lives in London and has two children.

Another book by Paul Theroux

LONDON SNOW

A
CHRISTMAS
CARD

PAUL THEROUX

Illustrated by John Lawrence

PUFFIN BOOKS

PUFFIN BOOKS

Published by the Penguin Group
27 Wrights Lane, London w8 5tz, England
Viking Penguin Inc., 40 West 23rd Street, New York, New York 10010, USA
Penguin Books Australia Ltd, Ringwood, Victoria, Australia
Penguin Books Canada Ltd, 2801 John Street, Markham, Ontario, Canada l3r 1b4
Penguin Books (NZ) Ltd, 182–190 Wairau Road, Auckland 10, New Zealand

Penguin Books Ltd, Registered Offices: Harmondsworth, Middlesex, England

First published in Great Britain by Hamish Hamilton Ltd 1978
First published in the USA by Houghton Mifflin 1978
Published in Puffin Books 1979
5 7 9 10 8 6 4

Made and printed in Great Britain by
Richard Clay Ltd, Bungay, Suffolk
Set in Monotype Centaur

1

WHENEVER I see light feathers of snow moving slowly down a window to make a white pillow on the sill, and hear the thin moan of wind through casement cracks in a room where a fireplace is singing with flames, I remember the Christmas when I was nine, and our house at Indian Willows.

We were lost. I knew that from the cold sound of my father's voice. He was angry, he shouted at me and then at my little brother, Louis. If he had known where he was he would have been confident and joked with us. We were in the family car, driving deep into the country. When the first snow started to fall and the car swerved on the icy road, Father hunched over the wheel and growled. The land was white and the sky dark. It was as if we were crossing a harbour at twilight. I was worried – because he was. I did not know what I could do to cheer him up. And the cold in the car's back seat made my fear worse.

It should not have been a desperate trip. Christmas was three days away. We were going to the house for the first time. My father, who was a traveller, had just returned from a journey in Asia. We had been delighted to see him, and for the early part of this trip to the country he had kept us entranced with stories of things he had seen – snake charmers, elephants trained to beg for rupees, and dancing bears. He had heard of a monkey which always travelled with a tiger, because the tiger was blind and needed the monkey to guide him. They were magical stories, and I felt that Father was touched with the same magic. The stories filled us with a longing to see such things, for it seemed that you had to travel across the world, through a wilderness of snow and fire, to know such enchantments – temples of gold, firewalkers and soothsayers, people vanishing in a puff of smoke.

Father denied this. 'You don't have to go all that way to know what magic is,' he said. As he spoke it began to snow. He smiled and said, 'What is magic? It is something being proven, not necessarily to make you understand, but so you will believe. The trick itself is a command, and the command is always the magician saying, "Believe in me!"'

We watched the snow falling. It gave the wind a billowing shape, like sheeted ghosts blowing towards us on the road.

'There is magic everywhere,' said Father.

'At our house?' asked Louis.

'Everywhere,' said Father. He tapped the side of his head with his finger, 'But it's mostly here.'

The house at Indian Willows was Father's surprise. He said it was his present to us for having waited so patiently for him to return. He had shown us a picture of it, taken on a sunny day in summer: a great barn-like building facing the ocean.

I examined the snapshot. 'Are there children there?'

'No neighbours,' he said proudly. 'Not a single one! It's miles from anywhere.'

I was sad. I had hoped there would be other children to play with. And so, even before we left our warm apartment in the city, I dreaded the vast wooden house with the dark windows and the green rooster on the weathervane. I didn't want to go, especially now, at Christmas, leaving everything behind. But Father insisted we would like the house. 'It has a fireplace,' he said. 'It's a huge old-fashioned one. We can chop some logs and build an enormous fire —'

It was the one image in my mind that gave me hope, the flaming logs in the stone hearth of the house at Indian Willows. I saw us gathered around this fire on a snowy night, until the image represented everything that Christmas was — light and joy. The fire assumed different shapes, changing from a bunch of plumes, to a sunrise, and then to a brilliant animal. To live in a house with a living fire — it was like having a tiger crouched in the wall of your room, yawning and flickering and blazing like a god.

We left the city on a cold morning. It was so early the street lights were still on, solitary yellow beacons in the empty avenues. We drove through the darkness like people escaping. We had brought a picnic lunch, which we ate in the parked car at the roadside, and all through lunch Father had studied a map while Mother fed us sandwiches. Later in the afternoon, on a narrow road (Father talking about magic), the snow began — first a flurry, then clouds of small sweeping flakes. With the snow it grew dark. The houses and stores we passed were shut, their windows unlighted, like blind eyes.

I said, 'Can we stop and buy something?'

I did not want to buy anything. I wanted to know why those buildings were deserted.

'Impossible. They're only open in the summer,' said Father.

Summer seemed so distant. The long drive and the winter cold were making me feel sick. I envied Louis, who was fast asleep and snoring, with his hands in his pockets.

'Why –?' I started to say. It was then that Father shouted at us to be quiet. Mother reached back and

stroked my hair. I knew that Father was lost. This made him seem angry, but really he was worried.

'There's a hotel,' said Mother.

'Closed for the winter,' said Father, and he swore. He did it forcefully, spitting out the words he told us we should never say.

The car slowed down. Ahead, through the snow tumbling in the headlights, I saw a fork in the road.

Mother rattled the map. She said, 'I can't figure this out.'

'Go left,' I said.

Father turned around and said, 'Why?'

The road on the left was wider. It had tyre marks and telephone poles and a very secure fence. It looked safe. But I did not know how to explain this. On wide roads I felt as if we were heading home, on narrower ones I doubted that we would ever arrive, and there were some small roads on which I felt we would disappear – just ahead – where the road seemed to end.

I said, 'Because there are signs on that one.'

'We've been driving for hours,' said Mother.

'I think Marcel has a point – about those signs,' said Father. He took the left fork. The snow was deep on this new road, and it was still falling. We were travelling down a tunnel that was white and collapsing softly upon us. The car slipped sideways and Father cursed. I was too afraid to move and warm myself. I prayed that we would arrive soon.

I had always trusted Father. He was funny, he was strong, he had made long and difficult journeys. But today he seemed different, somewhat confused by the snowstorm and uncertain of the road.

A storm to me then was simply terror and unusual noises. It was the pain in my toes from the aching cold, the stale smell of the car; it was delay. I was car-sick, I was impatient, I was sorry we had come. I had not really known why I had not wanted to leave home. Now I knew. The snow was relentless – it blocked the windows and made the wipers spank the frames. It was the reason we were alone on the road. We should not be here, I thought. This snow, these woods, this wobbling ride – it might never end.

And there was something else that I was almost too fearful to think: that my father – as reckless as he was brave – was doing something foolishly wrong, that he was misbehaving or breaking some law. He knew better than to lead us through this storm. But he had sneaked us away from home and now he was lost and so we were all lost.

Mother said, 'It's so dark – do you think we have far to go?'

'Ask Marcel,' said Father sharply. 'He's the one who told me to take a left.'

'Don't be childish,' said Mother. She often said this to him when he upset her.

'It's not far,' I said. I saw birds huddled in the trees at the roadside, roosting in the branches. This frightened me – even birds knew better than to travel in a snowstorm. And under each dark tree was a darker thing, like a panther, a sleek humpbacked shadow with its wicked face lowered in the snow, watching us pass.

'Look,' said Louis, waking and yawning, 'a light. Is that our house?'

'No,' said Father. 'But let's stop and get directions.'

The light flickered like fire.

'What is the light doing?' asked Louis.

Father was silent. He eased the car off the road into the driveway of a house so tall it rose like a chimney, upward into the stormy night. The snow appeared to fall from its upper storeys. It had a porch and an empty trellis, but its narrow windows glowed brightly and the light, as much a warning as a welcome, made it stranger than if it had been in total darkness.

Mother said, 'Is it a hotel?'

'It looks that way,' said Father. 'I can't imagine why it's still open. Maybe there's someone inside who knows where we are.'

He turned off the engine and walked towards the house through the troughs of snow. And he vanished inside.

2

WE waited in the car for Father to return. I said nothing to Mother, because I knew that if I spoke my voice would tremble. The wind had died and now the snow fell quickly and without a sound. There was no moon, but the windows of the looming house lighted the falling flakes and showed, in the yard, in the space between the nearby woods and the porch, odd humps and curves, as if bodies lay there on their backs, buried by the heavy snow.

All around the house the snow was both light and shadow, and far-off, white snow swooped from a black sky. I rolled the car window down a few inches and heard waves breaking. The sea was near, perhaps just beyond that grove of snow-covered trees. I wondered what happened to snow falling into the sea. The thought of icy waves and snow-flecked water riding across a deserted beach made me shiver.

The front door opened and paved the snow with a track of light. I saw Father, but he was not alone. At his side was a man much taller than he and wearing a crooked hat, and a black cape that seemed to give him limp wings, and leather boots that grunted as he walked. The man was brisk in his movements and rubbing his hands, and before he reached the car he was sprinkled with snow.

'Where are we?' asked Mother, as Father opened the car door.

'That's just what your husband asked me,' said the man, stooping to peer at me. 'What have we here? Two children? Don't sit there like a bump on a log – come in and get warm.'

'He thinks we should stay the night,' said Father.

'Absolutely,' said the man. 'I won't have you driving on these dangerous roads. Why, we're on the coast! One false move and you'll skid straight into the sea.'

'I'm sure our house isn't far,' said Mother.

'You'll know that tomorrow,' said the man, and began taking our suitcases out. 'Your husband said to me, "We're lost." Do you know what I said to him? I said, "You're not lost – you're at Osgood's."'

Mother took Louis in her arms and I followed in the narrow path of footprints.

'Right this way,' the man was saying. He went to the door and held it open for us. 'Just go into the parlour and put your feet up.'

As I passed him, the old man said, 'Mind if I call you Skipper? No? Well, look, Skipper, go in there and tell them not to worry. I won't bite them.'

The warmth of the house was perfumed with the odour of wood, as sweet as new blossoms, and the heat of the parlour stung my face. In a great square-shouldered fireplace a pile of logs blazed, and those same flames sparkled in mirrors and brasswork and crystal that filled the room. The lighted motion of the fire set shadows jumping and gave the paintings on the wall life and movement: a woman in one painting danced, a horseman cantered in a yellow field, a sly old woman in an apron dangled a key.

'Make yourself comfortable,' said the man to Father. He handed me a heavy poker and in a commanding voice said, 'Give that fire a push, Skipper.'

'I don't like them to play with fire,' said Mother.

I poked the logs and watched sparks scatter from them.

'He's not playing with fire,' said the man. 'He's helping it to breathe.'

The flames darted up the chimney and glittered in the man's eyes, and reddened his face as he watched with pleasure.

'We've got a fireplace,' said Louis. 'At our new house.'

'Where would that be?' asked the huge man.

Father said, 'Indian Willows.'

'That's two days' walk from here.' The man then excused himself saying, 'I'll be back in a jiffy.'

When he had gone, Mother said, 'I've never been in a hotel like this before. Or seen a hotel manager quite like him.'

'He said he's the caretaker.'

'What's his name?' I asked.

But before Father could reply, the old man entered the room again – he was still wearing his crooked hat and his black cape – and he said, 'Call me Pappy – everyone else does.'

Father said, 'Is this your hotel?'

'Who said it was a hotel?' said the old man. He placed the tray he was carrying on a low table, and set out slices of bread and a jar of jam and several long metal forks. 'These antiques are toasting forks,' he said, and stuck a slice of bread on the end of one. He showed us how to toast the bread by holding the fork near the flames, then he said, 'Now you do it,' and handed toasting forks to Louis and me.

'This is very kind of you,' said Mother. 'We hadn't expected to find anywhere open.'

'They're all closed,' said Pappy. 'But I'm glad to see you. No one's been here for quite a while.'

'So you do have guests,' said Father.

'Once a year,' said Pappy, smiling. 'About this time.'

Mother said, 'But where are they?'

'Right in this room,' said the old man with satisfaction. 'You.'

Then the only sound was the fire crackling in the hearth. The vast paintings on the walls still gleamed and shimmered, and the people in the frames watched us with bright eyes: a man in a chair hitched forward for a better look, the group portrait of a family stared wonderingly at us while their small dog wagged its tail. The horseman still cantered and the woman still danced, but their eyes were on us.

Just before Father spoke, I looked up, and it seemed that he and Mother were as handsome and attentive on their sofa as the people in those paintings. It was the effect of the fire, giving its lively beauty to the room.

Father said, 'Do you mean we're the first guests you've had for a whole year?'

Pappy nodded. 'The last ones left just a year ago. They spent the night – they were lost, too. This house is so far from anywhere that you have to be lost before you can find it. You're lucky, you know. People don't get lost much any more, what with the roads so straight. I mean, who gets hopelessly lost in the dark and the snow? You did – but you saw the light.'

'I've never been lost before,' said Father.

'That's what I mean!' said Pappy. 'Now aren't you glad you got lost tonight? If you hadn't, you wouldn't have found me.'

'So you're only open one night a year,' said Mother.

'I didn't say that,' said Pappy. 'I said people like you only stay here one night a year, the night that I'm on duty. Some years there's no one at all.'

'How very strange,' said Mother.

Father said, 'What do you do the rest of the time?'

'I admire the view,' said Pappy.

'Alone?' asked Mother.

'Madam,' said Pappy, 'do you really think you are alone in this room? Why look at all the people here!'

Saying this, Pappy did an unusual thing. He got up and reached into the fire and deftly removed a short stick. He swung it and a knob of flame gathered at its top, then he strode to the paintings with this torch.

'Judge Orpenshaw,' he said, and Judge Orpenshaw looked startled by Pappy's torch. 'Major McKay and his horse Lucifer. And there's the widow Pymore – people thought she was a witch with six fingers who hung in a chimney like a bat and howled. They blamed things on her.'

'Is that true?' I asked, chewing the jam-smeared slice of toast I had made.

'No,' he said. 'She only had five fingers, as you can see. Now there's the Grover family, and that thing that looks like a mitten is their dog Sammy –'

We watched Pappy as he crossed the room and held

his torch to the huge paintings and told us who the people were. As he spoke, the paintings became even more lifelike and when he finished it seemed as if we were in a room crowded with people who were silently keeping us company.

'What's that?' asked Father, pointing to a dark picture in the corner.

From where I sat I could see no more than a frame, a gold rectangle as tall as a man, elegantly carved. Inside this rectangle was darkness. It might have depicted a starless sky or dense fog or a cloud promising a night of thunder.

Father peered at it, 'I've never seen a picture like that before.'

Pappy said, 'That's not a picture.'

'What is it?' asked Mother.

Pappy had seated himself before the fire and tossed his torch into the flaming logs. He chuckled and said, 'If I told you that you'd know as much as I do.'

'If we're to get an early start tomorrow,' said Father, 'we'd better go to bed. We've got lots to do – Christmas is coming.'

'Christmas,' said Pappy, leaning forward. His voice rumbled in the room. 'You'll all be getting presents. But what if you could have anything you wanted – anything in the world? What would you say?'

'That's a tough question,' said Father.

'You say that because you don't know what you want,' said Pappy. 'You wouldn't ask for a miracle, really. You'd ask for something that someone else has – not something you'd imagined, but something you'd seen with your own eyes. And it would probably be very simple.'

'If I could have anything,' I said, 'I would say our house.'

'That's easy,' said Pappy. 'You already have a house in Indian Willows.'

'But we're lost,' said Louis.

'Wait till tomorrow,' said Pappy. Again he stretched his long arm and reached into the fire. Hovering near the flames he became a large red man in sorcerer's robes. He chose his torch and led us to the staircase. 'Now,' he said, 'I will show you to your rooms.'

At the top of the stairs he gestured with his torch. 'Children in there,' he said, 'and parents in there. I will say goodnight. And tomorrow you will have all the directions you require.'

A candle burned in the room Louis and I were to occupy, but even in that frail light I could see its strangeness. The ceiling was high and decorated, and the bed as wide as a barge, with bedposts supporting a fringed canopy. There was a red velvet sofa in the room, and a jug and basin, and a mirror I first took to be a painting.

Louis crept into bed and said, 'If I could have

anything I wanted in the world, I'd say jewels. Like Aladdin.'

I went to the curtains and drew them aside. The snow was still falling – it was deep on the sill. Though I said nothing to Louis, I could not imagine how in a place so buried in snow we would be able to find our house at Indian Willows.

3

DAWN was grey-blue, a smouldering spider in a cloud climbing to light other clouds. No sun – only this eerie light. The high black branches of trees were like antlers, and the lower branches wore pelts of new snow. All this we saw through frost which had etched fine shapes of ferns and flowers on the window panes of the bedroom. Louis and I had risen early, and the view outside was so strange we did not know where we were. Then we remembered the storm, the road, the house, and the friendly man who had welcomed us.

Instead of waking our parents we went downstairs, thinking that we might find the man. The house was still. Nothing stirred, though we heard – not far off –

the dissolving surf, waves sliding against the coast and the thin singing of wind in bare branches.

'Hello?' I called. 'Is there anyone here?'

My voice repeated and was returned to me from the wooden panelling in the hall and the depths of distant rooms.

Louis said, 'Let's look in the kitchen.'

'No, we shouldn't poke around.'

'But where's the man?'

'Maybe he's still asleep,' I said. Yet I had come downstairs fully expecting to see him, for he had said he would show us the way to our house today. I thought we might find him waiting in the front hallway. He was not there. I saw a bare coat-rack and a dusty moosehead and a Chinese gong. We tried the parlour, where we had warmed ourselves by the fire. The paintings were there, but the man wasn't, and there was no more fire. It had been swept clean and the firedogs were polished and the tray and toasting forks put away. It looked so neat it was hard to believe that it was the same room. Without the fire, the paintings were duller and I had never felt such a shrinking in my soul as when I realized the deception of those flat pictures.

'He's gone,' said Louis.

It was not exactly what I felt. I had the feeling that, though we might not find the man, he inhabited the house in some mysterious way. The house had a warmth that seemed to prove he was still around.

'Maybe he went out,' I said.

We crossed the parlour to the hall again and went to the front door. It was locked from the inside with a chain and a bolt. There were no footprints in the snow, either in the front or around the sides, for we spent the next few minutes looking out of all the windows.

It was when we were back in the hall and wondering what to do next that we saw the envelope. A white envelope, and large, it was propped against the ink-stand on a table near the coat-rack, as if it was meant for us – indeed, as if it was supposed to catch our eye. But there was no name or address on it, no stamp, no mark at all on the envelope.

Louis said, 'It's a secret message!'

'It's not much of a secret if it's out in full view where anyone can see it.' I picked it up. 'And it's not even sealed. Look, the flap is open.'

'Read it,' said Louis. 'I won't tell anyone you opened it.'

'I didn't open it,' I said. 'It was open already.'

I pulled out a card.

'What does it say?' said Louis, pawing impatiently at my sleeve.

'Nothing.'

I meant just that. There was no writing on it, only a stiff card, folded once, with a Christmas scene inside. I say 'Christmas scene', but it was more than that. It was a farm and marsh landscape seen from on high; a

bird's-eye-view of houses and trees sunken in snow, with roads traced around them, and the sea beyond. For a moment I thought it was a photograph, but when I looked closer I could see that it had been done down to the tiniest detail in pen scratchings that were so numerous and fine they appeared to have movement. The sea seemed to swell and the waves to nudge the shore, and I could see the vibrant blur of birds and chimney smoke. The style of this black and white picture was that of the paintings in the hotel – it was no style at all; it was lifelike. Looking down at this picture I looked down on a snowy landscape from hundreds of feet up, snowy roofs and roads that had just been ploughed and the shadows of tracks through the woods.

'It's a Christmas card,' Louis said. 'But it's not a very good one. There's no Santa Claus.'

'But you don't believe in Santa Claus,' I said.

Louis sulked. 'Well, there's no Jesus, there's no Christmas tree –'

'If you look hard,' I said, 'you'll see a nice white church – right there – and over there is a whole grove of pine trees. There's a Christmas tree, too.'

By squinting and putting his face very close to the card, Louis made out the church and the trees. But all he said was 'There aren't any decorations on that Christmas tree.'

'How could there be? It's in the woods, you nit-wit.'

'Let's show Dad.'

'He might get mad at us.'

Hearing footsteps, I slipped the card back into the envelope. The footsteps were loud and the sound shook the stairs. I backed away and was about to put the envelope on the table where I had found it, when Father appeared in his heavy boots and winter coat. He scuffed over to us and said, 'What have you got there?'

I showed him the envelope. He slipped out the card and studied it, then shook his head. 'It's rather a strange Christmas card.'

'That's what I said!' Louis made a face at me.

'Look what the kids found,' said Father. Mother had just entered the hall and, like Father, she was dressed warmly in her fur-trimmed hooded coat and boots.

'It's pretty,' she said. 'I wonder who it belongs to.'

'I think it's for us,' I said.

'There's no name on it,' said Mother.

'But we're the only ones here.'

'We can ask Pappy,' said Father. 'Have you seen him?'

'No – we looked everywhere,' I said.

'He must be here. He promised to give us directions.'

Louis said in small voice, 'Are we lost again?'

Father picked up the Chinese gong and punched it. The hollow *bong* echoed through the rooms, but when the sound died in a distant corner of the house, there was no reply.

'I don't understand,' said Mother. 'Where could he have gone?'

'There aren't any footprints in the snow outside,' I said. 'We looked.'

'We can't wait here all day,' said Father. 'We'll come back some other time.' Father went to the door and slid the bolt.

'Where are you going?' asked Mother.

'To the house.'

'How? Have you forgotten? We're lost.'

Louis looked desperate. He cried, 'We're lost!'

Father whispered a curse. 'And it looks as if we're snowed in too.' He paced up and down the hall. 'The least he could have done was leave us a note.'

I said, 'Maybe he left us this Christmas card.'

'I don't want a Christmas card,' said Father. 'I want a few simple directions to get us out of here!'

Mother said, 'Please don't shout. We'll find our way.'

'Of course,' said Father. 'We've got a whole day ahead of us. Let's get into the car and start looking. In the meantime, let's put that card back where you found it.'

'He'll be sad when he sees it,' I said. 'He'll think we didn't like it.'

Father said, 'Maybe we didn't,' and crossly scrutinized the card.

'He seemed a nice man –' I was saying. But Father interrupted.

'Hold everything,' he said. 'There's our house!'

We looked out of the window.

'Not there,' said Father. 'Right here, on the card. Look, see that big house with the weathervane in the clearing? That's our house.'

We looked on the card where Father was pointing. I could see the resemblance between this house and the one on the snapshot Father had shown us. But the snow in this picture simplified the house.

'There's the road I was looking for last night,' he said.

'Are you sure that's our house?' said Mother. 'This other one in the corner looks familiar.'

'No,' said Father, 'that one has a porch, and it's much bigger than ours.'

'The house we're in has a porch,' I said.

Father glanced out the window. 'Yes,' he said, 'this is the house we're in now. It's shown on the card! So all we have to do is go down that coast road and take a left and there we are. It will be about a two-hour drive. This is as good as a map.'

'It's better,' said Mother. 'Maps don't have houses on them.'

In the car, Father said, 'The first thing I'm going to do at the house is get a big fire going in the fireplace. You boys can help me get the logs. It wouldn't be Christmas without a fire.'

4

THAT was how we found our house at Indian Willows. It was a beautiful house – not the great gloomy barn I had feared, but an old solid farmhouse with a steeply pitched roof and a green rooster that spun on the cupola when the wind blew. The arrangement of rooms was topsy-turvy: upstairs was the kitchen and dining room, and a living room, which ran the length of the house; the bedrooms – four of them – were on the ground floor. The height of the living room, taller than the treetops, gave a commanding view of the sea – ten miles of blue ocean and the ice-covered curvature of coast. White caps teemed towards the beach, and standing at the window of the living room it was possible to believe that we were on the bridge of a ship and making for the open sea.

The fireplace in the living room was as Father had described it, an archway of boulders. As soon as we put our things away we piled logs in it and pleaded with Father to start a fire. Father was a methodical man. He would not light a single match until he was satisfied with the arrangement of logs, and underneath them he placed twigs and wood shavings which he said were necessary to kindle the fire.

'I want to light the first match,' said Louis.

'No,' said Father, 'I don't want you lighting matches.'

'Fires are dangerous!' said Louis.

So Father lit the first match, but it went out when he put it near the twigs. He lit another and another; he made a torch of the newspaper and poked it in. And the twigs caught and smoked. But the fire went out and the smoke entered the room and made our eyes water.

Father was not to be deterred. He tried again with shredded paper, and when that failed he used strings of bark. He coaxed a small flame from both the paper and the bark, but the flame was brief and the smoke suffocating.

'The chimney must be blocked,' he said. 'It's just as well.'

'Fires are dangerous!' said Louis again.

'You said it wouldn't be Christmas without a fire,' I said.

'The house is heated,' said Father. 'You're not cold, are you?'

'No,' I said, but I wanted to tell him that I had counted on seeing the fire roaring in the hearth like a tiger striped with flame.

Louis was saying, 'But if the chimney's blocked, how can Santa Claus get in?' and I was thinking with regret of the Christmas image in my mind, our family around the blazing fire like worshippers at an ancient ceremony, warming ourselves and rejoicing.

So we had no fire. For the rest of the morning I stared at the empty hole in the archway of boulders and at the cold logs Father had left in it for decoration.

During lunch Father said, 'Don't forget – Christmas is in two days. We've got to make some plans and get a tree.'

He talked excitedly – I suppose he was trying to take our minds off the failure of the fire – but what I thought of was Pappy and the hearth at his huge house and the way he had reached into the flames to select a torch. Father didn't mention him, but it was he who had helped us when we were lost, and it was his card that had guided us to our house.

'Have some more potatoes, Marcel,' said Father. Then, seeing that I was gloomy he added, 'What's wrong?'

'I was thinking about Pappy.'

'That old man? Yes, he was an odd one, wasn't he?'

'We should invite him to spend Christmas with us,' I said.

Mother said, 'That's a good idea.'

'I imagine he'll have his own arrangements,' said Father. 'He was strange. That story about his only having guests one night a year.' Father frowned. I could tell he doubted the old man's story. 'Then that Christmas card, if it *was* a Christmas card.'

'It *was!*' I said.

'It didn't say Merry Christmas,' said Louis.

'It got us here,' I said. 'If it wasn't for that card we'd still be lost.'

'That's right,' said Father. 'So let's hang the card over the fireplace.'

Because I had seen the card first, I was allowed to pin it to a ribbon on the mantelpiece. It dangled near my face. I saw the strange hotel we had stayed in, and I traced the various roads that lay between it and us. I looked closely at the woods that had so defeated Father's attempts to find our house, and I saw – about halfway between us and the hotel – a dark figure standing in a clearing in the woods.

'Look!' I said. 'That speck – that's the man!'

Louis squinted at it. 'I don't see anything.'

Father took the magnifying glass from my stamp collection and held it over the speck.

'It's a smudge,' he said. 'It's smoke.'

'It's not a smudge. It's a light – it's a man.'

'I don't see anything,' said Louis.

'He's standing in the woods,' I said.

'Why is he doing that on such a cold day?' said Louis.

'Maybe he's waiting for us,' I said.

Mother said, 'Those trees are rather dark.'

'Pine trees,' said Father still holding the magnifying glass. 'There's a big one – just the right size for a Christmas tree.'

'Let's go cut it,' said Louis.

'We can see the man at the same time,' I said.

Using the card to help us find the way, we headed towards the woods which lay alongside the salt marsh. But there the road ended, and we had to walk along a narrow path for some distance. We walked cautiously, glancing this way and that, for at any moment the man might run out from behind a tree in his crooked hat and his black cape. The pines were like tall robed figures watching us darkly from beneath jutting hoods, and one tree shook snow from its limbs and made Louis cry out, 'Dad!' For a time we seemed to be in wilderness, but soon we neared the clearing and I saw, just as it was shown on the card, the bushy pine tree we had singled out as our own. Night was falling and snow lay all around us, and yet the air was warm and the clearing itself had the quiet seclusion of a chapel.

Father lopped off the lower branches of the tree and then began cutting it with an axe.

Louis said, 'But where's the man?'

'I'm busy,' said Father 'You have a look.'

Mother and Louis set off in search of the man. I stayed in the clearing, holding the Christmas card. I did not search for the man in the snowy and now darkening woods; I looked for him on the Christmas card, where I had first seen him. But the speck had vanished and the card itself had grown dark.

When Mother returned with Louis she said, 'We couldn't find him.'

'I know,' I said.

'You didn't even look for him,' said Louis.

'Yes I did,' I said. 'I looked for him here.' And I showed him the card.

Father had started down the path, dragging the tree. 'Hurry up,' he said. 'It will be so dark soon you won't be able to see your hand in front of your face.'

Before I went to bed I hung the card on the fireplace once more. It seemed to me that the picture was darker and less clear than it had been, but the living room was not well lighted, so it was not easy for me to examine the card. Father was behind me, and I knew that he felt sorry for me. I had said the man had been waiting in the clearing, but we had seen no one.

'I know I saw him,' I said, turning around to face Father.

'It could have been an optical illusion.'

'The tree wasn't an optical illusion.'

Father said, 'Everything's so small on that card it's hard to tell what's there and what isn't. Sometimes you see what you want to see.'

'That's not true,' I said.

'Why not?' said Father. He spoke gently because he knew I was angry and disappointed.

'I want to see a fire in that fireplace, and I don't see one.' I turned my back on the cold cave-like opening and went up to bed.

There is a kind of silence that keeps you awake more than noise does. This silence made me think of the Christmas card. Father didn't believe what I had said. This seemed wrong, for if you didn't believe – or so I thought – the card might be taken away. When I couldn't stand it any more I got up, and so that I would not wake my parents I took a lighted candle with me, rather than switching on the lights. I used the candle to find my way.

My bedroom had been silent, but the house wasn't. I heard the squeak of the weathervane and the rustle of gulls on the roof and the swaying trees knocking their branches together with a sound like bones.

At the fireplace, the draught from the chimney chilled my knees. I held the candle up to the Christmas card, and in the uncertain flame could not make it out. I trembled and tried again: nothing. It was totally black, as dark as night. There was no picture on it, nothing but a disappointing pinprick of light in all that darkness.

I searched it for something more. I almost wept at the cruelty of it. There seemed something evil in the way it had vanished, and I went back to bed feeling very sad, as if a precious light had turned to dismal ashes.

What if you could have anything you wanted? The card, I thought, and then . . . then I was asleep.

5

IN my dreams, a flock of huge crows flapped from the burned limbs of leafless trees and massed over a snowy field. I woke in fright and saw that it was morning, but I stayed in bed. I did not want to see the dark Christmas card or be reminded of what we had lost. I could not bear to think that we no longer had a portrait of Indian Willows, the small world we inhabited. The card had shown us the house and the back roads. The man had worked his magic on the card: it was his gift to us. We had to value the gift for it to have meaning. But we had only thought of our Christmas tree and so the card had blackened with crows of doubt.

'You're a lazy bones,' said Louis. 'Aren't you going to get up?'

'No,' I said and pulled the covers over my head. 'I'm never getting up.' My experience in the night, holding the candle to the black card and seeing its darkness shimmering in the flame was like my bad dream, a nightmare I wanted to forget. And truly it was an experience of magic, for no sooner had I guessed that it was magic and tried to fathom the trick of it, than it had vanished, like the man.

Louis said, 'Don't you know what today is?'

'I don't care,' I said. And I thought: Poor Louis – he doesn't know about the Christmas card. He was excited, but before long he would know that it was now gone, as if the wings of great black birds had passed over it.

'It's Christmas Eve, silly,' he said. 'Tomorrow's Christmas!'

I wanted to tell him what had happened. But I could not think of any way to say it without disappointing him. He would not understand what I barely understood myself.

'We're going to decorate the tree,' he said. 'Please get up – it won't be any fun if you don't help.'

'I don't want to decorate the tree! I don't care about Christmas! Now leave me alone!'

My head was still under the covers. I heard the muffled noises of Louis getting dressed and thumping around the room. He left, banging the door, and stamped upstairs to the living room. It really was a topsy-turvy house: I could hear every sound he made, the way he paused at the living room door, and hesitated at the window, and his curious creaking steps as he crossed to the fireplace. He went a bit closer. There was a scrape, then a crash as he knocked the brass poker and shovel to the floor trying to get a better look at the Christmas card. There was a long silence, then two yelps: 'Daddy! Mummy!'

As he ran across the room, bumping into the chairs, I buried myself deeper into the covers. Louis headed downstairs, stumbling as he went, and he burst into the bedroom calling my name.

I held my breath. I didn't want to reply. I knew what he had seen.

'Marcel! Get up!' He jumped on top of me and began digging into the bedclothes and shouting. 'The Christmas card – guess what I saw!'

I tunnelled out of the blankets and said, 'I know what you saw – you don't have to tell me.'

'It's magic,' he said.

'Yes,' I said. 'But it's black magic. What good will it do us?'

'I don't know,' he said and he started to gnaw his finger.

I said, 'Now you've seen it, so you know. But I don't understand how the card could have turned black.'

'What are you talking about?' he said. 'The card

isn't black. It's the same as it was yesterday – I mean, almost the same. You said you saw it!'

'I did – last night.'

'Well, I saw it just now,' he said. 'And guess what? Do you know the speck we saw? It was so small yesterday I didn't really think it was the old man. But now it's bigger and clearer, and I think –'

I had jumped out of bed and dressed hurriedly, and before Louis could finish his sentence I dashed upstairs to the living room. The card was where it had been the previous night when I had seen it with my candle, still pinned to the mantelpiece. But today it was brighter than it had ever been, as sunny as the day outside our window. Louis was right – and he was right about the figure: there he was, not in the clearing where we had cut the tree, but on a back road. He was big enough for me to make out his crooked hat and cape and see that he was carrying something.

Louis said, 'What did I tell you? It's not black at all.'

'But last night –'

And then I knew: if the picture was really alive, an accurate picture of our world, then it would reflect cloud and sun; and if it was dark outside the picture too would be dark. I had seen the card at midnight, so I had seen only darkness. But with the dawn the picture had grown lighter and now it was as bright as morning.

Louis listened thoughtfully, still gnawing on his finger, while I explained this to him.

Then he said, 'It's a magic Christmas card! It shows day and night. It's not like a regular picture.'

'But it frightens me,' I said.

'Why? It even shows the man!'

'That's what frightens me,' I said. 'Look, there's the hotel where he lives. And there's the clearing in the woods where he was yesterday. And see where he is today?'

'On the little road,' said Louis. 'What's wrong with that?'

'Don't you see? He's headed in this direction – he's coming towards us!'

All this took place in the early morning, before Father and Mother got up. Over breakfast we told them what we had seen on the Christmas card – the movement of the man. I did not say that I had seen the card when it was black, because I thought they might be angry if they knew I had woken up in the night and used a candle to find my way to the picture.

Father said, 'You might be right, but remember what I told you about magic. It's mostly in the mind – you see what you want to see.'

'We're not imagining it,' I said.

'No,' said Louis. 'I saw it, too!'

'Get the card,' said Father.

I went to the fireplace and unpinned the card and brought it to him.

'Look,' I said. 'The man is on the road.'

I pointed to the road and heard Father chuckle.

'I don't see anything,' he said.

He was right; the man was not there.

'What did I tell you?' he said.

Mother said, 'It was probably a tree stump or a fence-post.'

'Or the shadow of a branch, or a boulder,' said Father. He winked at me. 'Or maybe you had something in your eye.'

'I didn't have anything in *my* eye,' said Louis and he looked fiercely at Father.

I could not believe that the man had disappeared. But he was not on the road, nor on the track near it where there was a cabin. Then I saw him: approaching the cabin he was clearer than ever. In fact, I could see that he was carrying a short stick in his right hand. I had missed him earlier because the bright sunshine had raked the snowy ground with vivid shadows.

'There he is,' I said. '*Now* do you think I'm imagining him?'

Father shook his head over the card.

'He's not there.'

'Near the cabin,' I said. I appealed to Mother. 'An hour ago he was on that road. Louis saw him, too. He's getting closer to us!'

Father smiled broadly and said, 'Maybe it's my eyes. Show me exactly where he is.'

I used the magnifying glass this time to focus on the spot near the cabin where I had seen him. 'Look carefully just beside the cabin,' I said.

But I looked before Father did: the man was gone.

'You see?' said Father. 'You're mistaken.'

'He's not there now,' I said. 'But he was a few seconds ago. So there's only one place he can be.'

'And where is that?' said Father.

I tapped the card. '*Inside* the cabin.'

6

IT was not until the middle of the afternoon that we were able to set off in search of the man. There was cleaning to do, snow to shovel, and of course the tree had to be decorated with bulbs and lights. It was a pretty tree, but even after it was lighted the chill in the room remained. I could not help thinking that it was the empty fireplace with its great gaping hole that made the living room so sombre.

There was no road to the old cabin. We travelled on foot through the woods. We had trouble locating the right path and it was already so dark that no other footprints were visible. The snow was luminous and made the woods seem unearthly, as if the treetrunks were floating a foot from the ground. We trudged in single file, Father leading the way. I was last in line, holding the Christmas card tightly in my mitten.

We were not far from our house. Only the woods and the expanse of salt marsh separated us from the cabin, but as there was no direct road it seemed a long hike. And we were walking slowly, for the moaning wind in the nearby trees appeared to warn us of what was ahead – perhaps danger in the gathering darkness.

Louis said, 'I don't like that screechy noise.'

'It's only the wind,' said Mother.

In the woods the wind has a kinder voice than in any city. The city wind is a sharp whine. It gusts through the street and tips barrels over and makes the street signs shudder. This was a soft sound, passing through the bare branches and seeming to mourn.

I looked up and saw the branches stiffen like the crows' wings I had seen in my nightmare. We entered a deeper part of the woods. Here, the trees swayed and the thin branches moved as delicately as a dancer's hands. But the sound of the wind made me freeze. It was a drawn-out wail which made the drooping branches rise and it showed us the way, pointing towards the darker woods with bony fingers.

'I don't see a cabin,' said Father. 'I don't think there is a cabin.'

'But there is – it's here,' I said, holding up the Christmas card. Yet the card was darkening because of the failing light reflected on it. And now it was not clear to me whether we were on the right path or going in the right direction.

'This is no place to be at this time of day,' said Mother. 'It's Christmas Eve. We should be home in front of the fire.'

I said, 'We don't have a fire.'

'I wish I was home,' said Louis sadly. He was just behind Father, and he stumbled forward kicking at the snow. He looked to me so rounded in his snow-suit — with his mittens and hood and boots — like a little lost bear cub.

A great shivering wind coursed through the trees and stopped us with its mournful sound. Father spoke, but he had to repeat himself before we could understand him.

'Of course,' he was saying. 'These are willows. Look how they lean over and sway.'

Each tree had a different voice, and together they sang like a choir.

Mother said, 'These must be the trees that give this place its name — Indian Willows.'

We were surrounded by the reaching branches of these trees. If I had been alone I would have been terrified.

I was about to speak. I turned, and what I saw took my breath away. It was a figure, deep in the woods, beyond the willows, highlighted by the snow. But even if there had been no snow I would have seen it, for it was a man carrying a flaming torch. It was no ordinary torch. It was a fountain of fiery gold, flaming in the distant trees and lighting the man who held it. He was moving quickly, blindly, towards the salt marsh, so the torch had the look of a comet, with streaks of flame tailing behind it. I had never seen anything like it, and for a moment I thought I was imagining it. Then I could only see the light, not the man, and I wondered if there really had been a man beneath it. The light was as brief as a falling star. I caught my breath and said, 'Look!'

'What is it?' said Mother.

'There – in the woods,' I said. Once again I thought I saw the light flickering where the marsh began, merely a whimper of flame through the trees. I tried to follow it with my eyes, but I lost it in the sunset glimmer that made bright creases in the pale sky.

The others were staring at me, as if I had gone temporarily crazy. It was too late to tell them what I had seen. Strangely enough, I had been cold before, and chilled by the wind, but the sight of that fire in the woods – that small comet of flame – warmed me. I was no longer cold or frightened. I could not help but think of the old man in the hotel and how he had used a similar sort of torch to show us the paintings.

'Let's go,' said Father at last. 'But if we don't see that cabin pretty soon, we'd better turn back. I'd hate to get lost here.'

I wanted to tell him that it was impossible to get lost as long as we had this Christmas card.

'Who wants to see a stupid old cabin?' said Louis. 'There's probably ghosts inside.'

'Don't worry,' I said. I was calm – not because I didn't believe in ghosts, but because I felt I had just seen one flickering in the woods, and it had not frightened me.

'The path's getting wider,' Father announced.

It was. The willows were much bigger, too. They had thick knobby trunks and each tree was like a great tent of overhanging branches pitched beside this aisle of snow.

Father said, 'Is that it?'

We looked ahead and saw a snug cabin set amid more willows.

It was not large. It was low – the sort of weather-beaten place witches inhabited in fairy tales, very isolated, on the far side of a broken fence, with a narrow front door and small crooked windows. Under the grey aching sky of nightfall – the smoky clouds cracked with light – the cabin had a shadowy haunted look. It was as moss-covered as a tree stump, and even in the biting cold had an aura of dampness, as if, lifting a floorboard inside you would find a family of wet toads huddled and staring up at you with glittering eyes. The cabin was a forgotten crate, a box of rotting timber and rusty nails, with a tarpaper roof, and only the snow and the willows

kept it from looking totally gloomy. I knew the moment I saw it that I did not want to go in. It made me think of wolves.

'I don't like that house,' said Louis.

Father said, 'It's strange, isn't it? Let's have a closer look.'

First we peered into the windows, but we could not see through the ragged curtains to the rooms beyond. We walked around the house and tried the back door. It was locked. We looked to see if there was smoke coming out of the chimney, but it was too dark to make it out. So we tramped around in the darkness trying to work up the courage to knock.

'I wonder if anyone's home?' said Mother.

Father prepared to knock, poising his knuckes over the front door.

'What will you say if they answer?' I asked.

'We can wish them a Merry Christmas,' said Father. 'After all, they *are* our neighbours.'

'You said we didn't have any neighbours,' I said.

'I guess I was wrong,' said Father. He knocked hard three times, and three raps echoed in the house.

I held my breath and waited. There was no reply.

'That's funny,' said Father.

Louis said, 'I want to go home.'

'Not so fast,' said Father. He turned the door-knob. It clicked and then he pushed it open. Now the darkness outside swept into the old cabin and the room matched the woods.

'What now?' said Mother.

Father shrugged and went in, and we followed at what we hoped was a safe distance. The cabin was dark, but it was not empty, for we bumped against chairs and tables, and from one of Father's sudden grunts I knew he had knocked his head against the low ceiling.

We felt our way through this first room. Then I heard the squeak of rusty hinges. Father had found another door.

'Come on,' he said. His voice was fainter than before. We hurried after him and in the darkness Louis took my hand. I thought some frosty ghost had snatched at my mitten. I let out a cry.

'It's only me,' said Louis, and held on.

This second room was, if anything, darker than the first, closer with the smell of decayed wood and termites and dead ashes. It was as if we were in an underground cavern and burrowing deeper, but our worst shock came when, after a few minutes groping here, we heard the terrifying bang of the front door slamming shut. That noise in the pitch dark of the cabin was like the door of doom sealing us in this place to die. I found it hard to breathe.

Louis sniffed a bit and then began to sob.

'Louis's crying,' I said. 'I think we should go.'

Mother said, 'The children –'

She was interrupted by tumbling voices; a low sound like the gentle moan of the willows, then a kind of hushed conversation – the crackle of two or three people speaking at once. In a lighted place the sounds might have been bearable; in the darkness of this cabin – which was much bigger inside than we had thought – the sounds were very frightening. And what were these sounds? They seemed to be those of prayer, the murmurings of kneeling people who were either very old or very young – not sad voices, but rapid joyful ones repeating the same simple phrases over and over. And in all this a child's crooning, an imitation of wind in winter branches. There was some laughter, and again it was dim and repetitive. They were human sounds but they were also sounds of rushing water or driving wind or snow falling fast.

'Here's another door,' said Father. His voice sounded distant and unpromising. 'Another room.'

I did not want to see the room and I could tell by the way Louis was clutching my hand that he did not want to see it either.

'Are you afraid?' he whispered.

I said. 'Yes, but –'

Father opened the door. Although we were nowhere near him, we knew he had done it, because there was a crack of light and then an explosion of warmth, as if he had opened a furnace door and let out flames. It startled me, and Louis stepped back and pulled me off balance. But Father was entering the bright room and saying, 'Well, glory be!' He sounded so pleased we followed him.

The room was long and lighted and there were

small brass pots on shelves and furniture shining with varnish. In one wall was a large brick fireplace with a roaring fire that filled the room with warmth and light. And the fire spoke: it chattered, it crackled, its many voices welcomed us and beckoned us forward. These were the voices we had heard, and the child's crooning came sweetly from the chimney. The fire was alive and as comforting as the one that had warmed us that night at the strange hotel.

'Isn't it beautiful?' said Mother.

'But where are the people?' said Louis.

'Maybe they just left,' I said. I saw that two chairs had been drawn up to the fire. The cushions had the look of having been sat upon; and there was a third smaller one, and a slight disorder in the room, as if the people expected to return at any moment.

It made me long for a fire of our own and regret that our chimney smoked and would not permit a blaze like this. But it had another look, too, which I could not quite express until Louis spoke.

He said, 'It's like a church.'

That was it exactly, for the chairs faced an altar of living flame that rose like prayer up the chimney, and the room narrowed towards the hearth like close chapel walls, so that merely warming ourselves in this way we were like worshippers and felt a great happiness. It was the relief of having come to no harm and the joy of just being there and facing the spluttering logs and the flames.

Whose house? Whose room? Whose fire? We had no idea, and yet we did not feel we were trespassing. Even more, we did not want to go back into the cold night to our house. And we were so engrossed in the fire, so comforted by the warm room, that it was not until the longest time that we remembered why we had come.

'I wonder if he's here,' said Father.

'Who?' said Mother.

'The man.'

Instinctively, I looked at the Christmas card. It was dark, as I guessed it would be – duplicating the night that had fallen outside. I looked closer.

Father said, 'He must have gone.'

There was no man on the card, but now I saw in the foreground a twinkling light. It was no larger than the head of a match. My mittens were secured to the sleeve of my coat with safety pins. I undid one pin and made a small hole in the card, in the spot where I saw the light.

'I hate to leave here,' said Father. The firelight made his face radiant, and his shadow leaped on the wall. 'But we have to go – what if we're here when the people come back?'

We lingered in the room. It was the strangest sight I had ever seen, a roaring fire in an empty house. I couldn't imagine anything more powerfully lovely.

7

ALTHOUGH it was Christmas Eve, our dinner was gloomy; we ate in silence. It had been hard to leave that warm cabin and return home to the emptiness of our own house and the sight of our fireplace with the dry logs stacked purely for decoration. At the end of the meal I asked Father to make one last attempt to build a fire.

'I'll give it a try,' he said.

The plumpest log in the fireplace Father had called 'the Yule Log'. He used everything he had to light it. He burned a lot of paper and all the twigs we had collected. He burned a pyramid of matchsticks, a handful of wood chips and a cup of kerosene. He fanned the dying flames with his slipper and blew until he turned red, then shredded his favourite magazine and threw that in. Finally, he sat down and watched the smoke trickling away from the cavernous hole of the fireplace. With a sigh the last spark died, and we stared at the cold ashes. Father's voice was glum with defeat when he said, 'It's no use.'

I had intended to hang the Christmas card over the fireplace in its usual position. But it was not until I took it out of my pocket that I remembered the pin-hole I had made in it. I examined the card and found to my amazement that while the pin-hole was where it had been, the small light had moved. Now it was nearer the foreground of the card. But as the card was dark I could not tell where the light was headed.

'Maybe it's not a light at all,' said Louis, when I showed him. 'Maybe it's just a breadcrumb that got stuck there. Or else a drop of the ice-cream you had for dessert. Maybe it's just a mess.'

'No,' I said. 'It's the same light I saw earlier.'

'Why isn't it in the same place?'

'It's moving,' I said. 'Like the speck we saw yesterday.'

'Your wonderful speck! The speck is on that card, but it wasn't in the woods and we didn't see it in the cabin.'

'We saw something stranger than that,' I said.

'Bedtime,' said Father. 'Brush your teeth and go to your room. And remember – tomorrow's Christmas.'

I got my safety pin and made a new hole in the card

where the light was, then hung the card over the fireplace. The bathroom door was locked. 'I'll be right out!' Louis said, but it was ten minutes before he unlocked it and another five before I put on my pyjamas.

Mother and Father were waiting for us in the living room. They kissed us and told us to go to bed. On the way I sneaked a look at the Christmas card.

The light had moved again. It was near my pinhole, but not through it. I made another hole and I had visible proof that the light was travelling in a straight line. How I wished that the card was not dark, so that I could see where this tiny star was going.

And yet in my heart I knew it was headed towards our house. I could not believe that it was wicked, but each time I thought of it moving towards us through the darkness I felt a cold fear in my body. It was closing in on us, and though it shone brightly it was hard for me not to think that this unknown light might do us harm. I hated to think this, but I did feel that in our house, in the snowy night-time woods, we were trapped. There was nothing we could do about it. Good or evil, the light would find us.

Father sat stiffly in his chair in the long chilly room. Mother was on the sofa. They said goodnight. The gaping black hole on the far wall under the Christmas card swallowed the echo of their words.

In the bedroom, Louis said, 'It doesn't feel like Christmas Eve.'

'Why not?'

'Because this doesn't feel like our house.'

I listened to him breathe in the dark.

Louis yawned. 'I liked that cabin.'

'I think that cabin was haunted,' I said.

'Even if it was – I'd rather spend Christmas there. It was nice and warm.'

It was what I had felt. I was going to tell him so. But within seconds he was asleep and snoring.

I could not sleep. I heard Mother and Father walking around upstairs. They were setting out our Christmas presents, as they did every year. Then, they went through the nightly ritual of closing doors and turning the lights off. I listened for more, the sounds of them locking up the house. The clank of bolts, the snap of locks: we were secure.

I slept, and I dreamed. My dreams were of the cabin. I saw a family which was much like our own, but with a small child in a basket. We lurked in their cabin, hoping we would not be seen. I dreamed I was alone in a dark forest, and all around me were the phantom lights of people I could not see, coming closer and circling like tigers' eyes. There was fire in my dream, like the fountain of gold flame I had seen in the woods. But when I dragged myself near it, it swept away and spilled like hot lava, melting the snow. The liquid fire destroyed the snow and made deep holes in the earth. I tried to run, because I was afraid of falling into a hole. I saw there were smoking holes all around me, and no path, no escape. I panicked and started to scream.

I heard a gust of wind, the slap of loose cloth, like a silk flag beating against a pole. This sudden gale startled me. It was no dream. The house shuddered like my heart. And although there was no rain or thunder, there were lightning flashes, the sort you see in summer skies, electric rips of sparks bursting at the windows. The slapping sound grew louder and I thought that the noise alone would tear the house down. It was the sound of a speeding bird's wings, but it was also the swift sound of flames beating in a strong wind.

More curious than frightened, I got out of bed, and guided by the lightning flashes I picked my way across the room. Each window was lighted and the blue flashes were as vivid as if the house had been borne into the sky, as if we tossed in a storm cloud supported by violent wind.

I heard no other sounds. I had left Louis asleep. The door to my parents' room was tightly shut.

Slowly, I climbed the stairs to the parlour. As I gained the top of the stairs, the lightning ceased, but not before I had a glimpse of a tall robed figure towering by the fireplace.

For a moment, in the darkness, I lost him. I clutched the banister and started to retreat. Yet I felt fascination quickening in me, and I returned to the top of the stairs for another look. I had learned not to fear the dark; and I did not fear this man. He was familiar: I had been expecting him.

All this took seconds – no more than that. The flap of his robe or cape was the flapping I had heard in my room. I could not see him very well, but I heard him turning in the darkness, the rustle and sweep of his thick clothes. As he turned, he produced a flaming torch from the folds of his cape and he held it aloft.

The flames made him huge and painted him with fire, like a sorcerer, and he filled that whole end of the room with the blaze of his torch and his flickering figure and the shadow of his tremendous size. If he had been no more than that, he would have seemed to me terrifying and powerful, but the firelight that made his figure gigantic gave his face a glow of fatherly gentleness. Like the fire he held, he was capable of destruction, and yet his magic was in destroying the dark and bringing light.

Until then, I had associated Christmas with tiny reminders of the season, plastic stars and toys and a tame fire in a hearth. Now I saw in this torch-bearer a different Christmas, not a one-day occasion for gift-giving and church-going, and not a sorcerer's trickery, but something fierce and everlasting, the strength of a hidden god who had reappeared to prove to me – clinging to the stair rail – that he could turn the world.

He moved and the room throbbed and the walls bulged and seemed to expand to contain his fire. The

torch-light made the house a palace and in this throne room he stood in the yellow-gold robes of a tiger king and beckoned me forward.

'Come closer, Skipper,' he said. I recognized the gentle voice. 'Don't be afraid.'

I hesitated. I did not feel fearful, but rather very small and insignificant. Why did he want me? I stepped from the stairs to the pool of brilliant light that lay across the floor.

'Closer,' he said, urging me.

I was now near enough to feel the heat of the torch, but it dazzled my eyes. I could not look directly at it, or at him. I watched the posture of his shadow on the wall, for it loomed over me like the man himself.

The shadow shifted. He reached to the fireplace, and now I saw that he held the Christmas card in his hand.

'I must take this away,' he said. He raised the card and its shadow covered the entire wall. 'What do you want for it?'

I shook my head. I couldn't speak. It wasn't mine – it was his. He had come to reclaim it.

Struggling with the words, I finally managed to say, 'It's yours.'

'No,' he said. 'You believed – you understood – so it became yours. But I need it now.'

I wanted to ask him why. I said nothing, but he saw the question on my face.

'To find my way back,' he said.

His shadow hovered.

'Will you help show me the way?' he said.

I must have looked rather frightened when he said that. I took a step back, but now he drew closer to me.

'You are not lost,' he said. 'You trusted the light, so you will never be lost again.'

He showed me the Christmas card.

'What will you take for it?' He spread his arms. 'You can have anything.'

Anything. My mind was a blank. I had been expecting him, but I had not expected this. And it seemed at that moment as if I had everything I could ever want, as if his very presence had made me a prince. Jewels, Louis had said; but jewels were merely an imitation of fire.

'Tell me what you want,' he said.

I could think of nothing solid. I thought of space and warmth and safety and happiness. Of not being alone. Of having a home and a family. Of love. There was no single thing that embraced all these, but only a perfect light, something indescribable, a flame. And though I tried, I could not speak. I stared past the man into the mouth of the fireplace, and I knew that it was that empty hole that I feared most: its cold draught and dead space.

The man seemed to know, without my saying so, what was in my mind. He lowered his torch and said, 'Take it.'

The torch burned brightly, without a sound.

'Light the fire,' he said.

The handle of the torch was within reach. I gripped it and as I did so I felt strength in my hand and that strength passed to my whole body. And then I knew the real power of that man, and while I held the torch I understood the innermost secrets of the world, for its light was wisdom and truth. And it was terrible, too, for in its power was the power to destroy. Its purity was heat and light mingled, darkness consumed to make fire – not the simple flame I had imagined, but something fiercer which, if not controlled and understood, was more deadly than darkness.

And now the man's voice boomed as he gestured to the fireplace with his muscular hand: '*There!*'

I moved the torch to the logs and the fire poured upon them and spread. The torch was taken from me, but I barely saw it, for the logs burned so brightly I had to cover my eyes. When I staggered back and uncovered them, the man was gone and there were only those leaping flames.

The fire spoke in the fireplace and the room filled with warmth. I crept near to it and watched it and believed that I saw the old man's face smiling in the shaggy flames. The room seemed very safe.

Dawn began to break across the seascape, another fire at our windows.

Louis came upstairs for his presents, but quickly

forgot them in his astonishment at seeing the fire. Father and Mother joined us at the blaze, and I noticed they were holding hands, like lovers.

'Your Christmas card,' Father said suddenly, glancing at the mantelpiece. 'Where is it?'

'I gave it back,' I said. 'I traded it for this.'

Father winked, as if he knew my secret. I think he believed that I had used it to start the fire. I suppose I had, though it had not happened the way he thought. I told him what I had seen, of the visit of the man who had come to reclaim his card. I did not say that I could have had anything in the world and that I had chosen this.

We did what is usual at Christmas. We opened presents and created a clutter of wrapping paper and ribbon and torn boxes. We ate our turkey and gave thanks for our good fortune. Throughout the day, the fire burned, holy and joyful, and it sang in the chimney like the voice of an angel.

8

Was there more? Yes. A week later we passed the hotel and recognized it and stopped. It was shut, but we saw now in daylight what we had missed before on that snowy night. There was a house nearby.

We inquired there, and a woman who gave her name as Mrs Pymore invited us in and offered us chocolate cake. We asked about Osgood's. Could we go in? It was closed, she said. Was there something special we wished to see?

'Pappy,' I said.

'The old man,' Father explained.

Mrs Pymore smiled. 'All right,' she said, and fished in her apron pocket for the key. She led us across the road to the house and inside the hall she paused under the moose-head and said, 'You'll find him right through there.'

The parlour was as we had left it before Christmas, just as neat and orderly, though not so warm. The fireplace was empty, the sunlight made shadows of the paintings on the walls. But I did not look closely at the furnishings – I was looking for a person, and I half expected him to appear at the far door and greet me.

Mother whispered, 'I don't see him.'

'Over there,' said Mrs Pymore. She used her key to point into the corner.

Then I saw him, and what I first took to be him stepping towards us from an elegantly carved doorway was his life-sized image in the painting that had been blank when we visited that snowy night. He was in his crooked hat and cape. He did not carry a torch, though in his right hand was a large white envelope.

'It's a wonderful painting,' said Mrs Pymore. 'He did it himself, and he finished it the day he died. I shouldn't say "He died" – it was more of a disappearance. And sometimes people around here claim to see him wandering in the woods – but only in winter, when this place is shut. This is a museum, but it used to be his house. It's even got beds upstairs.'

'We know that,' said Louis, but the old woman hadn't heard him.

'So he was a painter,' said Father.

'Yes,' said Mrs Pymore. 'He did all of these, but his self-portrait is the most mysterious. That's the one they whisper about.'

'What do they whisper?' I asked.

'That he could work magic,' she said. 'That his secret is in that envelope he's holding in his hand.'

'It might be a Christmas card,' I said.

'Nonsense,' said Mrs Pymore. 'You can see it's only a painted envelope.'

'No,' I said. 'I mean, inside the envelope.'

Mrs Pymore hunched and grinned and tapped my head with her key. Then she turned to Father and Mother and said, 'He believes the whispers!'

Also by Paul Theroux

LONDON SNOW

Wallace predicts snow and he is right. Overnight the city is transformed and to Wallace and Amy, Mrs Mutterance's adopted children, this mean tobogganing on teatrays – but the snow brings fear as well as fun. Mr Snyder, their mean and miserly landlord, disappears, and Mrs Mutterance insists that any human being, even one as horrid as Mr Snyder, is worth saving. So they all set off to look for him and trace his footsteps down to the river, but there the trail comes to an abrupt end. Could it have been foul play?

Some other Puffins

THE ROOT CELLAR
Janet Lunn

It looked like an ordinary root cellar, the kind of place where you'd store canned goods and winter vegetables. And if twelve-year-old Rose hadn't been so unhappy in her new home where she'd been sent to live with unknown relatives, she probably would never have fled down the stairs to the root cellar in the first place. And if she hadn't, she never would have climbed up into another century, the world of the 1860s, and the chaos of the Civil War . . .

MESSAGES
A collection of shivery tales
Marjorie Darke

How would *you* feel if you came face to face with a ghostly character on a Fun Run – or a flying broomstick with a mind of its own, a pony that keeps vanishing or a skeleton that is certainly not prepared to stay in the cupboard? These strange tales, and more, make up this spooky collection which will send shivers down your spine for sure!

THE LANDFILL
David Leney

Danny is angry when he discovers his safe, private world among the junk at the landfill has been invaded. But he has no idea that something as innocent as a story recorded on a cassette could have such a dramatic effect on his life.

ELEANOR, ELIZABETH
Libby Gleeson

Eleanor has been wary of her new home so far: the landscape is strange, the faces in the classroom unfriendly. Then, unexpectedly, Eleanor's lonely new life changes with the discovery of her grandmother's old diary. And then, with a bush fire rampaging just behind them, her life and the lives of Ken, Mike and six-year-old Billy depend on how she uses what she has learned about this alien world. She needs help, and only her grandmother, sixty-five years away, can give it to her.

A STITCH IN TIME
Penelope Lively

This seaside holiday is a time of finding things for Maria: names for birds and wild flowers, fossils in the Dorset rocks, a new friend Martin, a different Maria who likes noisy games as well as sitting quietly thinking. And a little girl called Harriet who lived in this holiday house a hundred years ago, and sewed an elaborate sampler – but why didn't she finish it?

MOONDIAL
Helen Cresswell

Minty has heard stories of strange happenings in the big house across the road from her Aunt's cottage. And when she walks through the gates, the lodge-keeper knows it is Minty who holds the key to the mysteries. She has only to discover the secret power of the moondial, and she will be ready to carry out the dangerous mission which awaits her . . .

A haunting and beautifully written time-travel novel, by the author of *The Secret World of Polly Flint*.

HAUNTING TALES

Ed. Barbara Ireson

Ghosts? No such things, you may be thinking. But this collection
has so many different ghosts, exciting ones, eerie ones, romantic,
sad and even funny ones, and they are all so vividly real that they
may well make you change your mind and become a ghost-fancier
yourself.

Barbara Ireson is well known as an editor and selector of anth-
ologies for children, and she chose these stories to appeal mainly
to readers of about ten to thirteen, though older readers will find
plenty to enjoy as well.

MOMO

Michael Ende

The sinister men in grey have arrived and are silently taking over
the city. They are drawing life-blood from the unsuspecting inhabi-
tants. They are the time-thieves. It is Momo, the ragged little waif,
who discovers what is happening. And it is Momo, with her un-
canny ability to listen, her simplicity and honesty, who holds the
key to salvation. She is the only one who can resist these soulless,
corrupt creatures. In this intricate and compelling story of a fantas-
tic country, Momo sets out to destroy the enemy, and the mysterious Professor Hora and his strangely gifted tortoise will help her.

TALES FOR THE TELLING

Edna O'Brien

In *Tales for the Telling* you'll meet giants and leprechauns, heroes
and princesses. Stories of love and high deeds which have been
passed from generation to generation are now presented together in
this colourful and charming volume. A huge tradition of Irish
storytelling is now available to a new audience.

THE WINGED COLT OF CASA MIA
Betsy Byars

'Mrs Minney, there is no such thing as a horse with wings. There never has been and never will be,' said Uncle Coot with all the authority of an experienced and thoroughly disillusioned stuntman, but alas for Uncle Coot, his neighbour's new foal most definitely *did* have wings, and she wasn't best pleased about it either.

Anyway, Uncle Coot settled the colt down on the ranch – as well as you *can* settle a horse that flies away if he gets scared – and it quickly became the centre of his nephew Charles's life. What hurt Alado the new Pegasus hurt Charles also, and through their adventures in caring for him, gruff Uncle Coot and romantic, bookish Charles began to make better sense of each other than they ever had before.

GHOSTS AT LARGE
Susan Price

A fearless soldier dares to spend a night in the haunted house over the Hell-crack, a pedlar makes a deal with the Devil, and St Peter visits the Underworld to quieten the rowdy dead. Meanwhile, a prince searches for the land of eternal youth, and the unfortunate Tom Otter for a riddle to save his life . . . Strange, eerie and startling happenings are afoot in every one of these compelling, traditional stories.

A TASTE OF BLACKBERRIES
Doris Buchanan Smith

The moving story about a young boy who has to come to terms with the tragic death of his best friend and the guilty feeling that he could somehow have saved him.

COUNTRY WATCH
TOWN WATCH
WATER WATCH
Dick King-Smith

An informative look at the natural world, written in a witty, anecdotal style.

HOW TO CATCH TIDDLERS
Ian Russell

A humorous, no-nonsense, extensively illustrated approach to tiddler-catching.

THE ANIMAL QUIZ BOOK
Sally Kilroy

A heavily illustrated quiz book covering all kinds of animals, birds, insects and reptiles.